Mermaid Magic
An Enchanting Story
of Secrets and Adventure

JeanAnn Taylor

Grateful Steps, 30 Ben Lippen School Road #107, Asheville, North Carolina 28806
Copyright © 2020 by JeanAnn Taylor
Library of Congress Control Number 2020945788 ~ ISBN 978-1-945714-20-7 Hard Cover ~ FIRST EDITION
Taylor, JeanAnn ~ *Mermaid Magic* ~ Illustrated by JeanAnn Taylor
Printed in the United States of America,
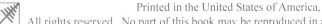
gratefulsteps.org

GREENLAND

NEW YORK

AMERICA

TEXAS

FLORIDA

MEXICO

HAWAII

An
Adventure
Around
the
World

Russia

France

Japan

Africa

Australia

"SophieGrace, it's bedtime." SophieGrace's mother peeked into her bedroom just as SophieGrace twirled one last time before she curtsied for her audience of dolls and teddy bears.

"Already?" SophieGrace asked.

"Yes, Greatdaddy will be right here to read a bedtime story to you."

SophieGrace picked up her favorite rag doll Rainy and climbed into her big canopy bed to wait for her great-grandfather.

SophieGrace loved her Greatdaddy. His skin was brown and tough from many years of fishing in the hot sun. His hands were calloused from hard work, and sometimes his back hurt, but his eyes lit up whenever he saw SophieGrace.

"What story shall we read tonight?" Greatdaddy asked as he walked into SophieGrace's room.

"The mermaid story," she answered.

"Ah, yes, the mermaid story." He picked up the book, sat down in the bentwood rocking chair, and began reading the familiar fairytale about a mermaid who fell in love with a handsome prince. Sunshine, the big fat orange cat, lay sleeping on a soft pink cushion as the chair rocked forward and back.

As she listened to the story, SophieGrace sleepily dreamed of being a real mermaid.

"And then, the mermaid princess and her handsome merman prince swam away to their castle in the sea." Greatdaddy closed the book and placed it on the table. "The end."

SophieGrace yawned and asked, "Greatdaddy, are mermaids real?"

"Of course they are," Greatdaddy answered.

"Why do they only live in the deep ocean?"

"Oh my sweet SophieGrace, mermaids have a lot of secrets. They live in many different places and can do things we humans can only imagine."

SophieGrace was skeptical. She turned up one corner of her mouth and raised one eyebrow. "How do you know that?"

"Well, SophieGrace, do you really, really, really believe in mermaids?" Greatdaddy asked.

SophieGrace yawned again. "Why, yes, of course." She blinked her eyes and sat up in her bed, her eyes growing bigger.

Greatdaddy took a deep breath and hesitated. "Okay, I'll tell you, but only if you promise to always believe in mermaids . . . and their magic."

Greatdaddy got up from his chair and walked over to the bookshelf. He picked up a sea-foam green, heart-shaped shell from the top shelf and held it in his hand. "You know, SophieGrace, I think it's time I tell you about the secret of this shell."

"Really?" she asked excitedly. SophieGrace knew there was something very special about the shell Greatdaddy had given her. He had told her to keep it in a very special place where it would always be safe.

Greatdaddy held the shell tightly in his hand as he pulled his chair a little closer and began to tell his story. "Well, SophieGrace, a lot of people think mermaids only live in the ocean. But, the first secret I'm going to tell you is that mermaids live in oceans, rivers, lakes, and even streams."

"How do you know that?" SophieGrace asked.

"Well, when I was a young boy, I grew up near a small lake in the Appalachian Mountains. It was surrounded by beautiful trees and flowers, and in the middle of the lake, there was a small island. On the island lived a family of blue herons. My two brothers and I fished nearly every day on that lake. We often caught enough fish for supper. In the summertime, we went skinny-dipping, but only when our mother wasn't home." Greatdaddy smiled and SophieGrace giggled.

"We always wanted to explore the island, but our parents would not allow it. They said it was too dangerous for us kids because there was a huge, mean snake that swam around the island. My dad said, 'That ugly ole snake thinks she's queen of the island.'

"Well, SophieGrace, you know how boys are. The more Mom and Dad said no, the more we wanted to go! So we began contemplating how we could get on that island without them ever finding out. The problem was we couldn't get there by swimming because the edge rose up too high out of the water. We knew the only way to get there was to build a raft so we could stand on it while we climbed onto the island. Of course, we had to do this without Mom and Dad catching us."

SophieGrace smiled. "Oh, Greatdaddy, you were bad!"

"Well now, SophieGrace, I wasn't really bad. I was just mischievous." Greatdaddy grinned back.

"So, my brothers and I began collecting nails and boards and rope from our dad's scrap pile. We hid our materials behind the big azalea bush down by the lake. Slowly and as quietly as possible, we built ourselves a right nice little raft.

"Finally, one hot summer day, while Dad was at work and Mom went off to her quilting group, we boys were home alone for several hours. We knew this was the opportunity we had been waiting for, so we put on our swim trunks and ran barefoot down to the spot where our raft was hidden. We dragged it to the water's edge and jumped on. We didn't have oars, so we used our hands to paddle to the island.

"Once we got there, we realized the edge of the island was three feet above the water. It was overgrown with weeds and vines, which made it nearly impossible to climb onto. But, we had worked so hard to build the raft and to get there, we weren't going to let a little underbrush stop us. After all, we were boys and we thought we were invincible."

SophieGrace rolled her eyes. "Boys always think that," she whispered to Rainy.

Greatdaddy chuckled and continued his story. "After studying the situation for a few minutes and paddling all the way around the island, looking for the easiest place to climb up, we decided to grab a vine and swing onto the island—you know, Tarzan style.

"Since I was the oldest, I decided to go first. We got as close as possible to the island, and I grabbed onto a low hanging vine. It looked strong enough to hold me and long enough to get me to the island. So I grabbed on tight and jumped off our raft.

"Unfortunately, I was wrong . . . on both accounts. First, it wasn't strong enough to hold me, and second, it wasn't long enough to get me onto the island. I fell hard and bumped my head on a rock. Then, I slid down the vine and into the water!"

"As I sank deeper and deeper, the strangest thing happened. Instead of getting darker, it began to get lighter. At first I thought I had hit my head so hard I was seeing things, but then I heard music and laughter. I felt the soft touch of a girl's hand take mine and pull me into a cave. Believe it or not, there was light and air in that cave.

   "I looked around, and I could barely believe what I was seeing. SophieGrace, there were mermaids there! Some were sitting together brushing each other's hair, while others were reading. Some were playing with dolls and some were dancing, but when they saw me, they all stopped and stared. They were very curious. I heard giggles and whispers, but I couldn't understand what they were saying."

"Real mermaids, Greatdaddy?"

   "Yes, SophieGrace. Now you would think that since I had bumped my head on a rock and sunk deep down into the water, I would have thought I had died and gone to mermaid heaven. And for a moment, that is exactly what I thought. But, I slowly began to realize that I had just discovered real live mermaids living in the very lake where I went swimming every summer!

   "The pretty mermaid who saved my life smiled at me. She had long, blond hair pulled to the side with a pink flower, a sparkly blue tail, and the brightest sea-foam green eyes I had ever seen. What happened next was like a dream . . ."

"That's quite an awful bump on your head," the mermaid said. She called for her little sisters, Paizley and Lyla, to bring witch hazel and cotton balls to her.

"My name is SparkleLeah. What is your name?" she asked as she patted witch hazel on my swollen noggin.

"Um-um-um. My name is Michael," I stuttered.

"And just what were you doing to find yourself in such a predicament?" she asked.

"Well, I-I-I really wanted to see the island."

"Oh, you must be careful! You know there are snakes up there!" she exclaimed. "Tiffany, the queen snake, is very evil. She swims around the lake to scare the birds and fish who come near. The only birds who aren't afraid of her are the blue herons. It's a dangerous place for boys."

"I know but . . ."

"No buts about it, the island is dangerous." SparkleLeah said emphatically.

"That's what my mom says," I told her. "Oh no! My mom! My brothers!" I suddenly remembered my brothers up on the raft. "Surely they think I've drowned."

"SparkleLeah, thank you for saving me, but I really must get back up to the raft to see my brothers."

"Okay then, let's get you back. But, Michael, you must promise to never tell your brothers about me and my sisters who live in this mermaid cave."

"But why? They won't tell anyone," I replied.

"No, Michael, I will only take you back if you promise not to tell," SparkleLeah insisted.

Greatdaddy took a deep breath and smiled at SophieGrace.

"So, I reluctantly agreed," he said. "I looked over at Paizley and Lyla. They had swum back to their mermaid dollhouse and were playing with their mermaid dolls. Then, SparkleLeah took my hand and led me out of the cave.

"When we looked up, we saw that mean snake circling the island. She was so huge a shadow of darkness came over us. We could hear her calling out, 'Hey ya'll. Where'd ya go?' I shuddered at the sound of her dreadful voice. We waited quietly until she passed by and went out of sight. I guess she went back to the bottom of the lake where it's dark and murky. Then, SparkleLeah led me to where my brothers were still sitting on our raft. They were in shock because I had just disappeared, and they were too scared to jump into the water to try and find me.

"When I popped my head out of the water, they both screamed my name and pulled me onto the raft. They couldn't understand how I had stayed alive under the water for so long. And I couldn't tell them. I couldn't break my promise to SparkleLeah. I looked around to see if SparkleLeah was swimming nearby, but she was gone. Just like that."

"Oh, no!" SophieGrace held onto Rainy so as not to let her disappear.

"After that day, we never got back on the raft, and we never tried to get on the island again. But I never forgot what happened or the pretty mermaid who saved my life."

Greatdaddy got up from his chair to stretch his legs. He walked over to the window and raised the lower pane to let the summer breeze blow into the room. Sunshine, who had jumped onto the windowsill, had been resting quietly. Annoyed at the new commotion, he jumped down and sauntered ever so slowly toward the door. When he reached the doorway, he turned his head to glance back at Greatdaddy and SophieGrace. Then, with the pompous air only a cat can muster, Sunshine left the room.

Greatdaddy shook his head. "That cat," he said as he sat down to continue his story.

"Years later, when I grew up, I decided to be a fisherman and get myself a nice big fishing boat. It was eighteen feet long, and I painted it sea-foam green, the color of SparkleLeah's eyes.

"I spent nearly every day on that boat: fishing and taking my catch to the market. It was a good life, full of adventure and salty air. I always wondered about the mermaid who saved me, but after so many years went by, I began to wonder if she had just been a dream. That is until one day while I was out fishing off the coast of Florida in the Gulf of Mexico.

"It was an especially hot day. I had caught a lot of fish and was just about to turn the boat around and head for land when I heard a woman singing. I thought I was hearing things and that maybe I had been in the sun too long, but then I heard my name!"

"Michael, Michael," I heard her say. I walked over to the edge of the boat and looked down into the water. I couldn't believe my eyes. After all these years, there was SparkleLeah looking straight up at me!"

"How are you, Michael?" she asked.
   "I-I-I'm well," I stuttered.
   SparkleLeah swam closer to the boat. "It's good to see you."
   "It's g-g-g-good to see you too," I stuttered. Again.
   "Would you like to swim with me?" she asked.

"Now, when I was in school, we learned about Greek Mythology and how sailors who had been out to sea a little too long thought they saw mermaids, or Sirens, as they called them. But when I saw SparkleLeah and heard her voice, I knew she was real. Still, I wasn't too sure I should actually jump into the water."

"SparkleLeah, I almost drowned once, and you had to save me. I don't want you to have to save my life again!"

"Don't worry, Michael," SparkleLeah said. "I'll take you on an adventure and introduce you to my friends. Then I'll bring you right back to your boat, and you can take your catch to the market."

"So, SophieGrace, against my better judgment and everything that made sense to me, I jumped into that deep water."
   SophieGrace gasped.
"Oh, Greatdaddy!"

"Now you would think I would have thought of this before jumping in, but it wasn't until I hit the ice cold water that this thought occurred to me, *How did SparkleLeah get from a lake in the Appalachian Mountains all the way to the Gulf of Mexico?*

"I was sure I had let my imagination fool me, and I just knew I was going to drown this time. So I closed my eyes and tried to think clearly. When I opened them and looked again, sure 'nuf, there was SparkleLeah with her bright smile, pink flower, sea-foam green eyes, and sparkly blue tail.

"SparkleLeah seemed to know what I was thinking. She swam up closer and said, 'Michael, you have proven yourself worthy of knowing the secrets of mermaids. I've waited all these years before talking to you again because I had to know I could trust you.'

"So, where have you been and how did you get from that lake in the Appalachian Mountains to the Gulf of Mexico?" I asked.

"'Mermaids have a lot of secrets,' SparkleLeah explained. 'Humans like to pretend they know us, but they don't.' With that she flipped her tail and dove into the water. When she came back up, she leaned in close to me and whispered, 'This is the biggest secret of all. Mermaids can fly. We fly from lakes to oceans, and from rivers to seas. I have many friends all over the world. Come with me, Michael, and I'll show you!'

"All of a sudden, I thought I was going to faint, and I began sinking into the water. Surely I was dreaming. I remembered the bump on my head from the first time I met SparkleLeah, and I thought I had relapsed and started hallucinating."

"But, SparkleLeah, I'm human," I pleaded. "I can't breathe under the water or up high in the sky."

"'I know that, Michael. This is another mermaid secret. You will breathe freely while we are on our adventure. Just close your eyes, kiss my lips, and the magic will come to you.'

"So, I took a breath and kissed her lips. Then SparkleLeah took my hand, and off we went."

SophieGrace was spellbound by Greatdaddy's engaging story, but it was getting very late now, and she was having trouble keeping her eyes open. "Close your eyes, SophieGrace, and I'll finish telling my story. You can imagine and dream about all the mermaids I met." Greatdaddy tucked the patchwork quilt under her chin as she snuggled under the covers and hugged Rainy.

She closed her eyes and listened as Greatdaddy's voice softly told her about his magical adventure.

America: Texas

"Since we are in the Gulf of Mexico," SparkleLeah said, "let's swim over to Texas where my friend Rosie lives." SparkleLeah took Michael's hand, and they swam across the Gulf as fast as a wink! They dove down into the water where they saw dolphins, king mackerels, tuna, and sailfish. Then, from a long way off, they could see a glimpse of another mermaid. And believe it or not, she was wearing a yellow cowgirl hat! She had a yellow tail and was riding a big, white seahorse.

"Rosie!" SparkleLeah called out. "Come meet my friend."

Rosie swam closer. She was eager to meet this human. "Howdy there! So, this is the buckaroo you saved a long time ago?" she asked.

"Yes, this is Michael. I'm going to take him all around the world to meet my friends!" SparkleLeah answered.

"Well now, you're in for a real treat there, mister," Rosie said with a distinctly South Texas accent. "Would you like to take a ride on Cowboy to start your adventure?" Rosie pointed to the seahorse she was riding.

Michael couldn't say no to that offer. Rosie slid off the seahorse and Michael jumped onto his back. Cowboy took him all around the Texas Gulf Coast Line, and then deep down into the water where they saw blue angelfish and orca whales. When they swam back to the top, they saw huge flocks of seagulls and pelicans fishing for their dinner. What a ride this was!

Finally, Cowboy took Michael back to where the mermaids were waiting.

"It's time for us to continue our journey," SparkleLeah said to Michael.

"Where are you going?" Rosie asked.

"We're going to a fiesta in Mexico. Rosie, would you like to join us?" SparkleLeah asked.

"Why, yes I would!" Rosie jumped on Cowboy and was ready to ride.

With Rosie riding Cowboy, and SparkleLeah holding Michael's hand, they swam swiftly through the deep water all the way to Mexico.

Mexico

When they arrived, they found the cave where the fiesta would be held. "There are many caves in Mexico," SparkleLeah explained, "but this is the most beautiful cave I've ever seen!"

They swam together through the large opening. It was so dark, they could barely see anything in front of them. Michael felt a little frightened and he wondered what he had gotten himself into. Finally, as they swam deeper into the cave and then around a bend, he could see the bright, cheerful decorations. Orange and red streamers hung from the top of the cave and swirled in the water. The tabletops were decorated with flowers and balloons. In the middle of the largest table was a big, beautiful cake.

As Michael looked around he thought, *It's festive-looking, but it's so quiet in here.*

SparkleLeah looked at Michael and winked. "It may be quiet now, but just wait." SparkleLeah seemed to always know what Michael was thinking. "We'll swim around the cave until it's time for the party to start."

Rosie, Cowboy, and SparkleLeah took Michael all around the huge cave. The water was so clear. SparkleLeah showed him where crystals grew and where unusual sea animals lived. Nooks and crannies were home to many sea creatures who never ventured far from their safe spot. Colorful plants grew and clung onto the rocks and sides of the cave. It was truly spectacular.

"Look, Michael! There on the rock." SparkleLeah pointed to a small, pink creature. "It's an Axolotl."

"An ah-what?"

"Axolotl. They are also known as, 'Mexican walking fish'."

"It looks more like a Mexican 'dancing' fish to me," Michael said as he watched the little creature swirl and tumble around in the water.

"Yes, it does," SparkleLeah laughed. "Axolotls are endangered amphibians, so we are lucky to see one."

Rosie, Cowboy, SparkleLeah, and Michael then swam back to the cave where a few mermaids were gathering. They watched as fish wearing large hats called sombreros arrived at the party scene.

Soon mermaids from all over Mexico arrived. They were dressed in bright colors with flowers in their hair and gold bangles on their arms. Little mermaids were wearing brightly colored skirts that swished and twirled in the water when they spun around.

"Ruby!" SparkleLeah called. "Come meet my friend, Michael."
   "Hola, Michael. I'm glad you are here!"

When the band arrived, the party really started. The music was lively and loud from the trumpets, violins, and guitars. Everyone was singing and dancing. Michael had never imagined such a merry party. "This is a festive fiesta!" he shouted over the music.
   "Come on, dance with me!" Ruby pulled SparkleLeah onto the dance floor. The two mermaids swung each other around and around until both fell on the sandy bottom laughing hysterically.
   Finally, after dancing and eating and laughing with her friends, SparkleLeah decided it was time to leave. "I'm exhausted. I think we should take a quick trip to Hawaii so we can rest." SparkleLeah said.

   "A quick trip?" Michael asked. "How do you take a quick trip to Hawaii, which is in the middle of the Pacific Ocean, when we are here in Mexico?"
   SparkleLeah, Ruby, and Rosie all looked at each other and smiled. "Michael, do you trust me?" SparkleLeah asked.
   "Well, SparkleLeah, here I am in Mexico with three mermaids. I don't really know how I got here or how I'm going to get back home, but, if I have ever trusted anyone in my life, I would have to say that it is you."

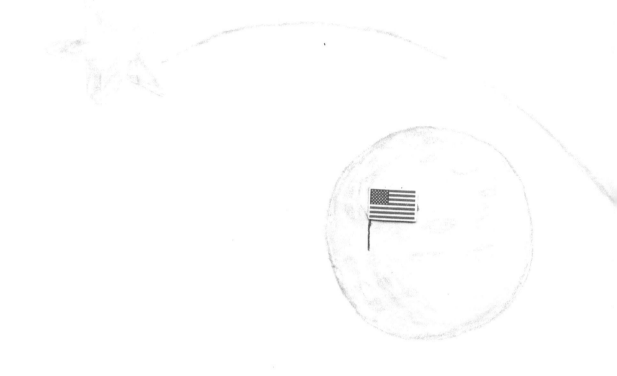

SparkleLeah smiled and took Michael's hand. They waved goodbye to Rosie, Cowboy, and Ruby as they swam out into the Gulf. Then, with a swish of her tail, SparkleLeah led Michael out of the water and up into the sky. They flew higher and higher, even flying above the clouds.

Michael looked at SparkleLeah with very wide eyes.

SparkleLeah winked. "I told you I could fly."

Michael looked at the moon. It was enormous and so bright! He looked down at the earth and thought it looked like a small, beautiful ball. He realized how tiny the earth is and how small we humans really are. It was truly magical.

Michael also realized that SparkleLeah could fly as quickly as she could swim. Which was very fast. In only a few minutes, he could see the islands of Hawaii on the horizon. As they approached the islands, SparkleLeah began to fly down closer to the Pacific Ocean.

"Who will we meet this time?" Michael asked.

"I want to introduce you to my friend Leilani. She lives in the Kaukonahua Stream, which is actually a thirty-three-mile long river with many twists and turns."

America: Hawaii

When SparkleLeah and Michael reached the very long river, he asked, "How do you know where to find her?"

"Leilani spends most of her day meandering along the stream and chatting with golden sunfish. She is a very friendly mermaid. I'm sure we'll see her soon. Or, we'll hear her." SparkleLeah smiled.

SparkleLeah and Michael swam along the winding river. There were flowers everywhere. Birds were singing louder and more cheerfully than he had ever heard. Butterflies flitted and bees buzzed from flower to flower, sipping the rich nectar. It was paradise!

As they swam around a sharp bend in the river, they heard a sweet voice singing a happy song.

> Oh Yellow Bird come sing with me.
> Sit down by my side.
> Oh Yellow Bird you sing so sweet.
> Tweet! Tweet! Tweet! Tweet! Tweet!

Michael looked up to see a pretty mermaid sitting on a rock and playing her ukulele. She had an orange tail and was wearing a lei made from orange and yellow hibiscus flowers.

"Hi, Leilani!" SparkleLeah called out. "This is my friend Michael."

Leilani smiled at Michael. "Aloha! I was just about to have a snack of this fresh, sweet pineapple. Would you like to join me?"

Michael hadn't realized how hungry he was until that very minute, but when Leilani cut the pineapple open, the fragrance of the delicious fruit filled the air, and they ate the whole thing!

"Let me introduce you to my friend, Tory," Leilani said. Michael turned and looked for another mermaid, but he didn't see anyone swimming around.

"No, silly, this is Tory." Leilani pointed below. Michael looked down and saw what was the biggest, hugest, most ginormous green sea turtle he could have ever imagined. At first, he was afraid of something so gigantic. He thought he might be the turtle's next meal. But Tory waved his arm in a gesture of friendliness.

"Let's go for a ride, and I'll show you the island," Leilani suggested. So, Michael and the mermaids jumped on Tory's back and went for a gentle ride through the many twists and turns of the river.

It was amazing. Tory took them places no human could ever go alone. They dove deep down to see coral and schools of brightly colored fish. *What fun*, Michael thought. *No one will ever believe this adventure I'm on!*

Although Michael would have been content to stay in the river with the mermaids and Tory for a very long time, SparkleLeah eventually said they should be leaving to go to their next destination.

"Where will that be?" Michael asked.

SparkleLeah excitedly clapped her hands together. "I have friends in Australia. Let's go there!"

From Hawaii to Australia. Michael didn't hesitate this time. He knew that while it didn't make sense to him as a human, it made perfect sense to SparkleLeah as a mermaid.

SparkleLeah took his hand, swished her tail, and off they went. They flew straight up out of the water and into the sky. This time they went higher, even going over the moon! The sky lit up with stars. It was a fireworks show Michael could not have imagined.

It was, in fact, a long way from Hawaii to Australia, but it didn't take a long time to get there. "We'll visit Olivia and Amelia. They live in a coral garden in the Great Barrier Reef," SparkleLeah said.

AUSTRALIA

Michael had never been to Australia, and when they reached the island, he was surprised at how large it was. They flew down into the Coral Sea, then swam to a small rock on the edge of the reef.

"Watch out for the dangerous tiger snakes," SparkleLeah warned Michael. "They're sneaky and will strike at you when you least expect it." Michael remembered the mean snake from the small island where he first met SparkleLeah, but then he shook that memory away.

"Oh look!" SparkleLeah exclaimed. "Koala bears!" Some of the cute animals were busily eating their seemingly endless meal of eucalyptus leaves, while others were sleeping in the trees. "They look so fuzzy and fluffy," she giggled.

"Do they ever come down?" Michael asked.

"Sometimes, and when they do, they can run as fast as a rabbit!" SparkleLeah answered.

As they sat on a rock, they watched kangaroos hopping along eating the grass that grew at the edge of the land. Michael and SparkleLeah watched for baby kangaroo heads to pop out of their mothers' pouches.

They enjoyed this nature show for a while before SparkleLeah said,
"Let's go see my friends. They're probably waiting for us."

Deep down in the water, they found the two mermaids swimming happily among the anemone with a school of clownfish. Michael was amazed at the bright, vivid colors of the coral.

"I've never seen anything like this!" he said.

As he admired the coral, he turned his head and suddenly saw a giant crocodile moving dangerously close to him. SparkleLeah swam straight toward the croc and looked squarely into his eyes. She quickly waved her hand signaling that he should leave immediately. The crocodile stared back at SparkleLeah. Michael wondered what was going to happen. Then, the crocodile slowly turned his head, and swam away in the opposite direction.

"Yikes! That was scary!" Michael gasped. "How did you do that?"

SparkleLeah smiled. "Well, let's just say that mermaids and crocs have an understanding."

With the dangerous crocodile episode over, SparkleLeah and Michael swam to where Olivia and Amelia were playing. As they got closer, Michael realized there were not only clownfish, there were also turtles and jellyfish and dolphins and starfish and sea urchins!

The mermaids and Michael played tag with the dolphins, hide-and-seek with the clownfish and had races with the turtles.

"SparkleLeah, this is the best time I've ever had," Michael said.

"Oh yes, Michael. But our adventure will continue in another land."

"Do we have to leave?" he asked.

"Yes, it's time to go," she answered. They said goodbye to Olivia and Amelia; then SparkleLeah took Michael's hand. Out into the sea and up into the air they flew.

"Where are we going?" Michael asked.

"I'm taking you someplace where you will see more animals than you can imagine. We're going to Africa," SparkleLeah answered.

Michael shook his head. "I've already seen more animals than I could have ever imagined!"

SparkleLeah smiled at Michael, and then up, up, up they went. They flew high above the clouds. Michael looked down and observed how some clouds appeared to look just like the ocean . . . or cotton candy. Some clouds looked like cupcakes and some clouds looked like dinosaurs.

"I have a friend who lives in Lake Victoria. Her name is Lulu, which means 'pearls' in her African language. She makes necklaces with pearls she finds in the ocean."

Africa

SparkleLeah and Michael flew down into the Kagera River leading into Lake Victoria. "I want to take you this way so we can see the hippopotamuses," she said.

Michael knew that hippopotamuses have a reputation for being aggressive, but after SparkleLeah had already saved him from a mean snake in America, and a giant crocodile in Australia, he wasn't too worried about a hippo in Africa.

It didn't take long to find a herd of hippopotamuses in the river. "They stay in the water where it's cooler during the day," SparkleLeah explained, "and then go on land to eat grass at night when the heat from the sun is gone." The hippos didn't seem to mind as they watched SparkleLeah and Michael slowly and quietly swim past them.

Suddenly, Michael looked up and saw a huge great white heron. It was standing on a rock in the river. "Look!" he exclaimed. "This heron is much bigger than the blue herons in the Appalachian Mountains!"

SparkleLeah agreed. "Oh, it is a beautiful bird! And there, on the other rocks are hundreds more!"

The hippos and herons were fascinating to watch, so SparkleLeah and Michael swam over to a small island and watched until the herons flew away.

"There are more animals to see before we meet Lulu," SparkleLeah said. "We'll swim over to Rubondo Island to watch the giraffes and elephants as they come to the fresh-water lake for a drink of water."

At Rubondo Island, there were many rocks to sit on while they waited patiently.

"Do you know that elephants are the largest land animal on earth?" SparkleLeah asked.

"Of course, I know that," Michael answered. "Everybody knows that. Do you know that giraffes have blue tongues?"

"Yes. Do you know that baby giraffes fall six feet to the ground when they are born?" she questioned him back.

"Yes. Do you know that elephants are the only mammal in the world that can't jump?" he asked.

"Yes. Do you know that giraffes are the only animal in the world that can't yawn?"

"Yes. Do you know that elephants can swim?"

"Yes. Do you know that elephants sing and purr like cats to communicate with each other?"

"Yes. Do you know that giraffes moo like cows?"

"Yes. Do you know that elephants hug their babies with their trunks?"

"Yes. Do you know that giraffes can sleep standing up?"

"Yes. Do you know that giraffes are so quiet, you can't even hear them when they walk in the jungle?"

This "do-you-know" game continued until all of a sudden, SparkleLeah whispered, "Shhh! Look up!"

Michael looked up and saw a giraffe walking in their direction. Then he saw another . . . and another. They were beautiful and so tall. Their graceful long legs brought them to the water's edge where they bent down to take a drink.

"Do you know that giraffes can go days without drinking water?" SparkleLeah smiled. "Okay, that's the last one."

"I wonder if we'll see an elephant," Michael said.

"Maybe, if we wait just a little longer," SparkleLeah whispered.

Then, just as the giraffes began to wander back into the jungle, a herd of elephants came walking to the water's edge.

"Look!" Michael said, "There they are!"

The powerful elephants were impressive to watch as they put their trunks into the lake to suck up the water and then pour it into their mouths. "Even though they are so huge, they seem gentle," Michael said.

"I agree. They are a special animal. Do you know that elephants remember their friends for their entire lives, even when they haven't seen each other for years?"

Michael just looked at her.

SparkleLeah smiled. "Oh, sorry. Last one."

They watched for several minutes as baby elephants splashed and played with each other. It was at once comical and cute.

"I think we should go now," SparkleLeah said. "Lulu will be waiting."
   They slid down from the rock, and then just as they were about to dive into the water, they heard a sharp, shrill sound. They looked up to see chimpanzees swinging in the trees.
   "Well, SparkleLeah, you were right. I could never have imagined all of these animals!"

When the chimps finally left to swing back into the depths of the jungle, SparkleLeah and Michael dove into the water and swam deep down into the lake. They found Lulu sitting on a rock, making a necklace with her newest collection of pearls.

"Oh, how pretty!" SparkleLeah said as she swam to where Lulu was sitting.

Lulu looked up. "Hello," she said to Michael. "SparkleLeah has told me about you. It's very nice to finally meet you. Would you like to make a pearl necklace?"

Michael shook his head. "I don't know how to do this," he answered. "It looks complicated."

"Don't worry, I'll make one for you," Lulu assured him.

Lulu picked up one pearl at a time, strung it onto a silk cord and tied a knot. She continued this process until she had a long strand of pearls, each one separated by a tiny knot. When she was finished, she handed the necklace to Michael.

"It's really quite beautiful," he said. "Thank you, Lulu!"

"Keep the necklace until you are ready to give it to someone truly special."

Michael agreed and gently placed the pearl necklace safely in his pocket.

"Michael, it's time for us to leave now," SparkleLeah said.

Michael and SparkleLeah said goodbye to Lulu, once again swam out into the water and then flew up into the sky.

Japan

"We're going to the Sea of Japan to meet Sayuri," SparkleLeah announced. "Her name means 'Little Lily,' and she is the tiniest mermaid I know."

They met Sayuri at her enchanting, tiny home. SparkleLeah and Michael squeezed awkwardly to fit into her small space. Inside, Sayuri displayed her collection of kokeshi dolls. Michael had never seen this type of doll before.

"Please sit down and have a cup of ginger tea with me," Sayuri said.

"That would be delightful," SparkleLeah answered.

They sat down at the tiny table where Sayuri served tea to them in tiny tea cups. As they sipped their tea, Sayuri explained the story of the kokeshi doll. "They are all handmade from blocks of wood by artists in Japan. They have round bodies and heads. Their colorful kimonos are painted with charming flowers and birds. Some even have little umbrellas attached to their side."

When they finished their tea, SparkleLeah said, "Why don't we take a swim through the Sumida River so Michael can see the cherry tree blossoms?"

"What a lovely idea!" Sayuri answered. "But I know of a secret river where there are not so many people. Let's go there."

Sayuri picked up her tiny lace-trimmed parasol and very elegantly led her friends out into the sea. They turned into a quiet, secluded river lined with hundreds of pink cherry trees. The blossoms reflected on the water, creating what looked like a pink tunnel.

"Oh, my!" SparkleLeah exclaimed. "This is beautiful. It looks like the whole world is pink!"

"It does, Sayuri! Thank you for showing this special place to us," Michael added.

As they swam along the river, captivated by the beauty, Michael thought about this magical journey. *I wonder if I can stay forever.*

Once again, SparkleLeah seemed to know Michael's thoughts. She answered by saying, "Sayuri, this has been lovely, but we must continue on our journey."

SparkleLeah and Michael waved goodbye. "Please come for tea again soon!" Sayuri said as she bowed respectfully to her guests.

Michael reached out and took SparkleLeah's hand, fully trusting that wherever and however they got to the next place, it would be magical.

"Where are we going next?" he asked.

"We're going to France." SparkleLeah answered. "It's just exquisite there, and I want you to meet my friends, Chantilly and Eyelet. They're fashion designers. They have fairy fingers and make beautiful, ornate shell tops and tiaras"

"Mermaid fashion designers?" Michael asked.

"Yes! They are quite well known in the mermaid fashion district. But first, we're going to fly over the lavender fields of Southern France."

FRANCE

From the sky, they could see lavender blooming across the horizon. Many of the fields were lined with sunflowers, making for a colorful and extraordinary view. The sweet, delicate fragrance rose up and filled the air. Michael was completely mesmerized.

SparkleLeah flew down closer to the flowers. "Close your eyes and take a deep breath," she said as they flew slowly over the field. "Try to hold the moment in your mind."

They lingered over the flowers to feel the serenity and peacefulness from the fragrance. Then they quietly continued their journey to the Mediterranean Sea. Looking down, they could see the beautiful, turquoise blue water.

As they flew to the Côte d'Azur, also known as the French Riviera, they found the two designers busily stitching pearls and crystals onto silk fabric.

SparkleLeah and Michael quietly swam toward the busy mermaids.

"Oh, Chantilly, this is gorgeous!" SparkleLeah exclaimed as she swam to where Chantilly was working. Chantilly held up a top covered with colorful periwinkle and aqua marine crystals in a swirly design.

"Thank you, SparkleLeah," she answered.

"This is my friend Michael. We're on an adventure." SparkleLeah explained.

Chantilly and Eyelet put their work down for a few minutes to chat with their guests. I'm making a special outfit for the princess of the sea. Eyelet is designing a tiara for her to wear to the Mermaid Ball.

"It's beautiful." Michael said. "I'm sure she'll love it!"

"Okay, that's enough chit-chat," Chantilly proclaimed.

"Back to work," Eyelet added.

SparkleLeah and Michael wished them well and swam back into the sea. Then, with one flip of her tail, SparkleLeah guided Michael out of the water and back up into the sky.

AMERICA: NEW YORK

They quickly flew across the Atlantic Ocean to the Hudson River near Manhattan to meet Arabella. While in flight, SparkleLeah warned Michael, "Arabella just loves to dance, so don't be surprised if she asks to dance with you."

"Does she dance like Ruby?"

"No, she swims around in tiny twirly circles like a ballerina," SparkleLeah answered. "She loves ballet so much she gives dance lessons to the starfish!"

When they got to the river, they dove into the water and could clearly hear Arabella's voice. "*Plié* and *relevé*! Now, *piqué*, *piqué*, and *passé*!" There were several starfish standing in a straight line. All were pointing their toes and doing their best to follow her instructions.

When Arabella saw SparkleLeah and Michael swimming toward her class, she clapped her hands and dismissed the starfish. "Come back in twenty minutes," she said.

The starfish leaped away to a soft, sandy spot where they could sit and rest their tippy toes.

"Hello, Arabella!" SparkleLeah introduced Michael to Arabella, and then to no one's surprise, Arabella looked at Michael and asked, "Michael, will you dance with me?"

Michael looked at SparkleLeah for help, but SparkleLeah just smiled. Then, Arabella turned up the music, took Michael's hand and began twirling. Before he knew it, Michael was dancing . . . under the water . . . with a mermaid.

Of course, Michael had danced with girls before, but he always felt awkward and wasn't sure what to do. Now, with Arabella, he felt as free and confident as a real dancer! He spun her around the river bottom as if he had been dancing all his life.

Arabella loved it. "Oh, Michael, you must come back and dance with me again!"

Michael bowed and said, "It would be an honor, my lady."

SparkleLeah couldn't help herself. She laughed out loud at the formality of the two dancers.

Then Arabella clapped her hands, calling the starfish back to their ballet class. As SparkleLeah and Michael swam away, they could hear Arabella calling out steps to the starfish. "*Tombé, pas de bourrée, glissade, pas de chat!*"

GREENLAND

Michael was still out of breath from all the dancing as SparkleLeah took his hand and led him out to sea.

"Our next stop is Greenland where you can meet my friend Addie."

Michael seemed worried. "Greenland? It's freezing there!"

"Yes, Michael. It is cold there. In fact, Addie lives in the Arctic Ocean where the water is so cold it turns to ice."

"Isn't she cold?" he asked. "Won't we be cold?"

SparkleLeah winked and said, "Oh, Michael, don't worry."

They swam out into the sea for several miles before she swished her tail, taking them out of the water and up high into the vast, dark sky. Then, as they flew back down toward the ice-covered island, Michael felt the temperature drop, but strangely enough, he didn't feel cold.

SparkleLeah guided Michael down through the clouds. "What is that noise?" Michael asked as he held his hands over his ears.

SparkleLeah pointed to a large group of white birds. "It's the snow geese." They watched as thousands of beautiful white birds flew toward the water's edge to search for a meal of seeds, roots, and leaves.

Then SparkleLeah and Michael dove back into the icy water. Michael was sure he would freeze, but once again SparkleLeah was right. He didn't feel too cold at all. In fact, he felt warm and perfectly comfortable. As they swam through the Arctic Ocean, they came upon a herd of ice seals. Michael, having never been this close to a seal, was fascinated.

"These seals are called 'ribbon seals' because of their ribbon-like patterns," SparkleLeah explained. "This is quite a treat, Michael. Humans rarely have the opportunity to see a ribbon seal!"

Leaving the seals behind, they continued on their journey and were soon surrounded by enormous black and white orca whales. Michael thought back to the crocodile episode, so only slightly afraid, he held tightly onto SparkleLeah.

SparkleLeah realized that Michael was frightened. To assure him of their safety, she explained that orcas are actually gigantic dolphins. They are also extremely smart animals who know that mermaids are magical and should be treated with respect. So, there was nothing to worry about. As Michael and SparkleLeah swam by, the orcas acknowledged the swimmers but stayed at a polite distance.

"Michael, do you believe in unicorns?" SparkleLeah asked slyly.

"I guess so," Michael answered skeptically. "I know mermaids are real, so I guess unicorns are real too."

"Look over there." SparkleLeah pointed to a pod of whales with long tusks spiraling out of their heads.

"What are those?"

"They are narwhals, the unicorn of the sea. They love cold water—the colder the better! They mostly swim under the ice. Listen to their whistles. That's how they communicate."

SparkleLeah slowed down so they could get a better look at these amazing creatures.

Watching the narwhals left Michael speechless. His thoughts took him from riding a giant seahorse in Texas, to watching giant whales with unicorn-tusks in the Arctic Sea.

As they continued on, Michael remembered visiting a zoo as a young boy. There, he had watched penguins hop off an ice block and splash into a pool of water over and over and over again. "I hope we see penguins," he said.

"We won't see any today because we are in the Arctic, which is in the northern hemisphere. Penguins only live in the Antarctic, which is in the southern hemisphere. A lot of people get that mixed up. But you will meet Addie's pet polar bear Penelope."

"A pet polar bear?" Michael shook his head. "Addie has a pet polar bear? Can I pet her? I bet her fur is soft."

"I bet you think she has white fur."

"Well, yes. All polar bears have white fur."

"Actually, her fur consists of clear hollow tubes filled with air for insulation from the cold. Her skin is black to help absorb the sunshine and to stay warm. The clear tubes appear to be white so that she can blend in with the snow. And yes, you can pet her. She's a very sweet bear."

Michael shook his head. He was always amazed at SparkleLeah. She seemed to know everything!

When they arrived at Addie's igloo, SparkleLeah introduced Michael and then asked, "Where is Penelope?"

"I have a surprise for you!" Addie answered. "Follow me."

Addie guided SparkleLeah and Michael to a snow den just around the bend. They quietly swam inside.

"Shhh," Addie said. "They may be sleeping."

Shhh...
Baby
Sleeping

SparkleLeah and Michael peeped into a small room where Penelope and a tiny bear cub lay cuddled together sleeping soundly.

"Oh!" SparkleLeah gasped. She could hardly contain her excitement. "Penelope had a baby?"

Addie smiled with sheer delight. "Yes, her name is Pippa, and she is absolutely adorable." Addie held her hands to her heart. "We just love her!"

"Oh, can I hold her?" SparkleLeah eagerly asked.

"Maybe," Addie answered. "They sleep twenty hours each day. Baby Pippa is still hairless and only weighs one pound, so Penelope is quite protective of her."

"I understand," SparkleLeah said. "Perhaps next time when she is a little older."

Addie laughed. "Yes, she'll soon be running amok as all little bears do."

Michael and the mermaids swam back to Addie's igloo where they enjoyed a cup of hot chocolate and graham crackers together.

After a while, SparkleLeah said just what Michael had come to expect, "It's time to go."

Addie swam with them to the top of the icy water and then blew kisses as the two flew off to another land.

Russia

"It's just a hop, skip, and jump—so to speak—to our next stop."

"Where is that?"

"Russia."

SparkleLeah and Michael swam across the Arctic Ocean. "Before we meet my friend Svetlana, we'll fly above Moscow so you can see buildings that look like onions."

"Onions?" Michael was intrigued.

They flew just high enough to observe the colorful buildings with tops that really *did* resemble onions.

"These are beautiful! So many colors and patterns. Why are they shaped like onions?" Michael asked.

"There are many reasons, but one is so that snow can't accumulate on top. It simply slides down the slope," SparkleLeah answered.

After several minutes of sightseeing, they flew on to Lake Baikal. "Svetlana lives in this beautiful, freshwater lake. Because it's so special, it's known as the Pearl of the World. The water here is exceptionally clear, extremely cold, and it's the deepest lake in the whole wide world. Svetlana is a chamomile flower gardener, which is the national flower of Russia."

When they found Svetlana, she was busily tending her garden. She looked up over the patch of daisy-like flowers when she heard her visitors approaching, "Hello! I'm almost finished picking this bouquet."

Michael and SparkleLeah swam to the spot where she was picking fragrant flowers and watched as she placed them into a woven basket.

After their introduction, Svetlana said, "I'm going to make chamomile tea. Perhaps you would like a cup?"

"Of course!" SparkleLeah and Michael answered together.

When Svetlana finished her task, they followed her to her home where she steamed a pot of chamomile blooms to create a delightfully aromatic brew.

SparkleLeah sipped her tea and took a deep breath. "Oh, Svetlana, we've been so many places. It feels wonderful to rest for a few minutes."

As Michael looked around Svetlana's home, he noticed her collection of matryoshka dolls and remembered his grandmother's own nesting doll collection, and how he played with the wooden dolls when he was a young boy.

He quietly sipped his tea and thought about Sayuri's kokeshi doll collection in Japan. He also thought about how Ruby and Arabella both love to twirl and dance. He remembered the pretty pearl necklace Lulu made and the fashion designs from Chantilly and Eyelet. He thought about Rosie's pet seahorse, Leilani's pet turtle, and Addie's pet polar bear. He remembered the peaceful feeling of the lavender flowers in France and the similarity of the soothing chamomile flowers in Russia. As he thought about all the places he had traveled and all the mermaids he had met, he realized how different each place was, and yet how very similar.

When SparkleLeah said it was time to go, Michael wasn't surprised. They thanked Svetlana for the chamomile tea and off they went.

"SparkleLeah, this is the most amazing journey," Michael said. "I've seen so many beautiful places and met so many wonderful new friends!"

"Yes, and you are going to love the next place we'll visit. It's actually our last stop and near where your boat is waiting for you."

Michael had forgotten all about his boat and his catch of the day. He didn't even know how long he had been on this journey. "SparkleLeah, I don't know if I want to go back. I think I want to stay with you and this magical adventure forever."

SparkleLeah looked at Michael wistfully, and then with a cheerful voice said, "We're going to Weeki Wachee, Florida, which is near the Gulf of Mexico."

Michael silently imagined the long distance between Russia and the Gulf of Mexico. *I wonder if we'll swim or fly,* he thought.

"Let's take a swim," she said, as if she knew what he was thinking, again. "We'll see hundreds of fish and maybe a great white shark as we swim around the Atlantic Ocean to the gulf side of Florida."

"A great white shark?" Michael said. "I can go without seeing a gigantic shark like that."

"Don't worry, Michael, they don't usually come too close." She winked.

Michael knew he was safe with SparkleLeah so without hesitation, off they went. SparkleLeah held Michael's hand as she took him back down through the cold, deep water of the Arctic Ocean and into the warmer water of the Atlantic Ocean. They swam past jellyfish, stingrays, swordfish, dolphins, and giant whales before seeing a very large, great white mama shark swimming with her little baby shark by her side. "Baby sharks are called pups. Isn't it cute?" she giggled.

Then, just as SparkleLeah had predicted, the mama shark just winked at them as they swam past.

America: Florida

"Weeki Wachee is a funny place because humans there think they know all about mermaids." SparkleLeah laughed. "They even think mermaids want to become human! Can you imagine?" She laughed again.

Michael knew of many fairytales about mermaids who dreamed of becoming human. But now he knew that a mermaid would never want to give up the freedom of flying, swimming, and having friends all over the world.

As they swam around the tip of Florida, SparkleLeah decided to fly the rest of the way. So she took Michael's hand, swished her tail, and up they went. When they got just above the tiny town of Weeki Wachee, they saw the tourist attraction where people from all over the world came to see the mermaid show. They peered down to see hundreds of tourists lined up and waiting to watch the underwater, spectacular exhibit. "There is a spring nearby where we can swim and play with my friends, Piper, Emma Claire, and Annie," she said as they flew down to the water.

Across the spring stood hundreds of beautiful pink flamingos, eating their shrimp supper while standing on one leg. They looked as if they were practicing their ballet lessons. *Arabella would like to see this,* Michael thought to himself.

As SparkleLeah and Michael arrived closer to the spring, they could hear squeals and laughter. The mermaids were playing hide and seek with giant manatees. When the manatees found the mermaids hiding in the shallow caves, the mermaids swam to the top, letting the bubbles from the spring tickle their noses.

"These manatees are as big as elephants," Michael said.

"Yes, they are. That's because manatees are water cousins of elephants." SparkleLeah explained. "Many years ago manatees were mistaken for mermaids by sailors who had been out to sea for a long, long time. Of course, you know better thán that." SparkleLeah winked at Michael.

SparkleLeah and Michael flew down and watched as the mermaids and manatees played.

Michael, would you like to swim with the manatees?"

"Of course!" he replied.

SparkleLeah and Michael dove into the water. As Michael swam closer to the manatees, he realized just how huge, yet gentle, these animals are. The manatees very slowly glided through the water. They seemed to enjoy the game of hide-and-seek as much as the mermaids and Michael.

"These quiet giants are really just big lovies," SparkleLeah said.

Again, Michael was having so much fun he didn't want to leave. Yet again, SparkleLeah finally said it was time to go. Sadly, Michael said goodbye to the mermaids and their manatee friends.

SparkleLeah looked at Michael with her pretty, sea-foam green eyes. "This is the end of our journey today," she whispered.

"But I'm not ready to go back. I want to stay and travel around the world with you!" Michael pleaded.

"No, Michael. Your life is on land with your family. They need you. We'll always be friends, and you'll always be in my heart."

Michael knew she was right, but that didn't make it any easier to say goodbye. "I'll always remember you as well, SparkleLeah. Thank you for this amazing adventure." Then, he reached into his pocket and pulled out the pearl necklace Lulu had made and given to him. He placed it over SparkleLeah's head.

SparkleLeah blinked back a tear and handed him a sea-foam green, heart-shaped shell. "Keep this as a charm to remember our adventure," she said. "Remember the sky we flew through, the stars and the moon. Remember the mermaids, Tory the turtle, Cowboy the seahorse, and Penelope the polar bear. Remember the magic, and remember me."

SparkleLeah took Michael's hand as they slowly swam toward his boat. She kissed him on his forehead, and then suddenly he was sitting in his boat, surrounded by the catch just as he had left it.

Michael shook his head. *Did that really just happen?* he wondered. It must have taken several days to go around the world and swim with all the mermaids. But when he looked at his watch, it showed that only minutes had passed. He wasn't even going to be late for the market. He must have fallen asleep and had this wild, whimsical dream!

He was just about to brush it all off when he suddenly saw the heart-shaped shell on the floor of his boat. He picked it up and held it in his hand. He knew SparkleLeah and the adventure had been real, yet he decided not to tell anyone. He knew his friends and family would think he was crazy or that he had, in fact, been in the sun much too long.

So, he cranked up the engine and headed for land. As he started his ride back, he felt someone looking at him. He turned around just in time to see a sparkly blue tail slip into the water.

Greatdaddy took a deep breath. "Mermaid magic. That's what it is. That's the only explanation for what happened."

SophieGrace sleepily opened her eyes. "Greatdaddy, will you ever see SparkleLeah again?"

"I don't know, SophieGrace. Maybe. Or maybe not. But I know she's out there somewhere."

"I'm glad you came home, Greatdaddy." SophieGrace reached her arms up to give Greatdaddy a hug.

"I am too, SophieGrace. I am too."

SophieGrace looked at the shell still in Greatdaddy's hand. "Greatdaddy, is that the shell SparkleLeah gave you?"

"Yes, SophieGrace, it is. I want you to keep it and always remember this magical mermaid story—and the secret of the shell."

"I will!" she promised. SophieGrace hugged Greatdaddy again and then kissed him goodnight.

Greatdaddy got up from his chair, placed the shell back on the top shelf, and turned off the light. He walked over to the window and looked up at the moon. He wondered where SparkleLeah was on this warm summer night. Then, just as he was about to walk away, he saw something. He watched as a shadow slowly glided across the moon.

The shadow wasn't ugly or scary like a witch. It was rather pretty and elegant like a mermaid. He imagined that SparkleLeah was flying across the sky. Maybe she was on her way to ride Cowboy with Rosie or dance with Arabella or visit Penelope and Baby Pippa with Addie.

Greatdaddy didn't know if he would ever see SparkleLeah again. But, he could always dream about their adventure and remember the magical time he flew around the world . . . with a mermaid.

Author's Note

Mermaid Magic has taken me on a long journey. From places I'm familiar with to places I'm not likely to see. When I began, I never dreamed it would take five years, many tears, countless re-drawing and re-painting of the illustrations, a lot of money, and lots and lots of patience peppered with tenacious determination to make my dream a reality.

The story itself came pretty easily—as if by magic. I began with a vague idea of the mermaids, their locations, and their storyline. Then, as I sat at my laptop, the book manifested in a way that can only be described as spiritual. When my story was finished, I began a search for an illustrator. I interviewed several talented artists, but quickly realized that my vision was too precise and clear to let anyone else take over with her own interpretation. One artist said she didn't like authors to dictate what she could draw. It was then I knew I had to illustrate my book myself. I remember the day I bought expensive colored pencils.

The cashier asked, "Are you an artist?"

I looked at her and replied, "I'm trying to be."

She looked right back at me and said, "Own it."

What I ended up owning was a mess. As hard as I tried, I could not make these mermaids express my vision. Months and months later, I serendipitously discovered watercolors. I knew this was the right medium, but now I had to learn another technique. While drawing and painting animals came pretty easily for me, facial features of people were painfully challenging. I struggled to draw eyes, noses, and chins. It was tedious and not always fun. My determination and drive to succeed was the only thing that kept me going. Although it seemed to take forever, very slowly and one page at a time, the illustrations began to reflect my vision. Reward began to replace despair, satisfaction replaced hopelessness, and finally one day this book was finished. I know the images are not perfect, but it's my best work—for where I am right now.

Throughout this long process, my publisher Micki Cabaniss Eutsler was with me. She patiently edited the text and constructively criticized the illustrations. Without Micki, this book would not have been possible—and the world would never know the truth about mermaids.

I learned a lot from writing and illustrating this book, but the one thing I learned above everything else was to trust myself—my intuition, my vision, my dream, and my journey. So to all the mermaids around the world I say ~

Follow Your Heart, Follow Your Dreams, and Stay in Your Magic

Growing up in Florida, JeanAnn could swim practically before she could walk. Her infatuation with mermaids grew as she spent many summer days "playing mermaid" in the community pool. After a family trip to Weeki Wachee, Florida, to visit the mermaid tourist attraction, JeanAnn began imagining a world where mermaids were truly real. *Mermaid Magic* is the result of a fantasy that never went away.

Author JeanAnn Taylor is an independent writer of fashion, style, and life-reflections for local magazines. Her first children's book, *The Little Girl Who Loves to Twirl*, was published in 2011. JeanAnn is an avid needle artist with interests in crochet, embroidery, quilting, doll and dressmaking. She is also a passionate dance competitor who placed in the 2020 Country Dance World's Championship.

JeanAnn lives in the beautiful mountains of Western North Carolina where she finds inspiration in quiet mountain tops and bubbling streams.

CPSIA information can be obtained
at www.ICGtesting.com
Printed in the USA
BVHW052357240521
606871BV00001B/2